Creative and delightful! The author's clever twist on common themes is brought to life with illustrations that capture the reader's imagination. Children will adore the dog theme, while adults will be reminded of times gone by. Add this book to your list of must-read magical adventures!

-- Reviewed by Karen J. Laggner M.Ed.

Kim, your collection will do wonders for young developing minds. Kaileigh, our daughter, an animal lover and someone who is an aspiring young artist, absolutely loved it! Your short poems and beautiful art work was perfect for the level she can comprehend. We know your first edition will be a success and we look forward to more special editions from you.

-- Reviewed by Renee, Ryan and Kaileigh Masterson

If you're a dog lover, don't miss this charming book. Wonderfully illustrated with limericks. Spoiler Alert: Author is an artist and has painted many pets. Great inspiration; will be picking this up as a gift for several of my friends with furry children.

-- Reviewed by Patricia Saporito

Amusing, lively, unpredictable moments in the playful lives of the animals we all love is captured in this book. Kim Esposito is a "twinkle in her eye" observer and imaginative artist whose charming cartoons and quotable ditties will appeal to all ages.

-- Reviewed by Lois, MSEd

Sky diving dogs, surfing dogs, ears in the wind. I feel like a kid again, ready for anything. This book is not just for children, as it fired my own imagination! Yep 8 to 80 years old will love it and ask for more.

-- Reviewed by Sylvie Meyers

A Special Book For
You And Your Pet.

Follow me on a dog's journey: Free in a world of no cages or boundaries...
A magical place, where our beloved furry friends are unleashed. Who knows,
maybe your pet will be a part of this growing adventure... Or already is? by espo.

Pet Tales

Inspired from dog rescues and puppies I raised. Each pet tells his or her own story.

Kim Esposito

Unleashed Melody

Four couples dance on a moonlight ships, floor.
The Dalmatian turns his head and lets out a proud roar.

The ship moves gracefully with its waves all around,
While the dogs dance to a peaceful sound.

The Boarders

Louie and Freckles snow board high in the sky,
Their fur twisting and twirling as they fly by.

With not a care in the world they spin around
Over the snow covered mountains they have found.

Rodeo Hound

Hear the crowd roar! It's Rambo the rodeo hound.
He hangs on tight as the bull pounds the ground.

Our fearless Chihuahua is king over the bull.
Audiences gather together: the stands are full.

Quick and courageous, don't blink an eye,
As Rambo gets tossed high in the sky.

The Howl Club

Duke the Doberman wins the game.
He does a back flip and enjoys his moment of fame.

His brother Donald lets out a howl and a bark.
No one likes to lose at golf and be left in the park.

Pete the Pug never has a chance
While his flipping buddy continues to dance.

Canine Fever

Levi the Shepherd levitates with his dirt bike beneath him,
He soars high in the sky over a tree limb.

Flying alongside him are four birds in the air.
We wonder if our brave canine will win the dare.

His buddies cheer him from below with, "Good luck!"
Landing back onto the ground, he hopes to miss the duck!

Big Dog

A sunny summer day with the smell of ocean air in the winds
Dancing beside the rustling and swaying palm tree limbs.

Bernie the Bernese Mountain Dog is cruising on the beach side
While looking for a sweet little pup to join him for a ride.

Amped

Pitsee the Pit Bull, our water loving surfer,
Rides the giant waves without a life preserver.

She wonders about what lurks way down under
As that huge wave crashes around her like thunder!

Daring **Dalmatians**

Penny and Pepper hike up the mountainside
Not looking at the sharks circling below, hungry and alive.

Someone's screaming, "Look, there's smoke and perhaps a fire!"
Their curiosity has their attention as they climb up higher.

Our fearless pups have rescued the day!
They put out the smoking leaves and saved the bay!

Tail Spins

Colleen our Collie stands at the water's edge flying her kite;
The wind twirls it up higher as it takes flight.

Dobie the Doberman is flying his beside hers.
The summer breeze lifts it wildly as it stirs.

Rottie the Rottweiler chooses her own sunny path,
Pulls in her kite to jump in the lake and take a bath.

Air Hound

Our military hounds are trained to serve and protect.
Only the finest do they select.

Jumping from the airplane to the ground below,
This Weimaraner is putting on quite the show!

Supported by his buddies who are next to jump,
There will be applause as he lands with a thump.

Ruff Play

The stadium comes alive as our pups make the final play.
Who will catch the football and win the game today?

Butch, the fearless Pit Bull, tackles from behind
Ray the Rottweiler is over the winning line.

The crowd roars as the touchdown is made.
Ray catches the ball; well played!

Bone Appétit

Izzy and Winnie are enjoying a bowl of bone soup.
Fine dining on a secluded island for this little group.

They enjoy a day out in each other's company;
The drink is refreshing and quite bubbly.

Colorful glasses of red and green
Go along beautifully with the ocean scene.

Zoey's Vespa Ride

Zoey speeds along the seaside on her ride,
Smiling with the wind in her face, full of pride.

While making a left or a right, it's hard to decide.
Perhaps she'll take a break and park on the side.

Or maybe she'll cruise along the road statewide.
It is quite the day for a joy ride!

Design, illustrations and narration: Kim Esposito
www.designinlivingcolor.com

Follow Kim on Instagram:
pettales2021.

Kim and Levi at his first vet appointment.
He was 4 months old. 3/3/2020